BOYZ RULE!

Pirate Attack

Felice Arena and Phil Kettle

illustrated by
Susy Boyer

MONDO

First published 2003 by
MACMILLAN EDUCATION AUSTRALIA PTY LTD
627 Chapel Street, South Yarra, Australia 3141

This edition first published in the United States of America
in 2004 by MONDO Publishing.

For information contact:
MONDO Publishing
980 Avenue of the Americas
New York, NY 10018

Visit our web site at http://www.mondopub.com

04 05 06 07 08 09   9 8 7 6 5 4 3 2 1

ISBN 1-59336-362-1 (PB)

Library of Congress Cataloging-in-Publication Data

Arena, Felice, 1968-
    Pirate attack / Felice Arena and Phil Kettle ; illustrated by Susy Boyer.
    p. cm. -- (Boyz rule!)
    Summary: Jamal and Joey play pirates in the back yard, climbing aboard
    Joey's father's new boat. Includes simple sailing facts and questions to test
    the reader's comprehension.
    ISBN: 1-59336-362-1 (pbk.)
    [1. Pirates--Fiction. 2. Boats and boating--Fiction. 3. Play--Fiction.] I. Kettle,
    Phil, 1955- II. Boyer, Susy, ill. III. Title.

PZ7.A6825Pi 2004
[E]--dc22

                                                                2004042699

Project Management by Limelight Press Pty Ltd
Cover and text design by Lore Foye
Illustrations by Susy Boyer

Printed in Hong Kong

Contents

Jamal   *Joey*

CHAPTER 1

High Sea Dreaming

Best friends Jamal and Joey have been told by Joey's mother that they should go outside and play.

Jamal "Whoa! Look at that! It takes up the whole backyard."

Joey "Yeah, it's Dad's new boat.
He got it last week. Cool, huh?"

Jamal "Yeah. It's huge!"

Joey "I know, we're lucky. Dad's
dreamed of owning a boat all his
life. And now he does."

Jamal "Hey, it'd make a great pirate
ship."

Joey "Yeah, I guess so."

Jamal "Hey, imagine if we were pirates. We could capture all the treasure in the world and sell it."

Joey "Yeah, that'd be cool. But why do you think pirates' treasure always turns out to be jewelery?"

Jamal "Maybe they have lots of girlfriends?"

Joey "Gross."

Jamal "Yeah, if I was a pirate I'd want to get bikes and CDs and stuff like that—things I could use."

Joey "So, wanna go on board my dad's boat, I mean, our pirate ship?"

CHAPTER 2

Captain 'n' Crew

The boys go out into the backyard
and climb onto the boat.

Jamal "This is so cool!"
Joey "Raise the anchor and prepare
to set sail."

Jamal "Who made you captain?"

Joey "Okay, well maybe we could both be captains?"

Jamal "Good idea. I wanna be 'Captain Blood.' The most feared pirate in the world!"

Joey "Cool. Then I'll be 'Captain Splash.'"

Jamal "That's a weird name for a pirate."

Joey "Well, if anybody tries to board the boat, they'll see how scary I look."

Jamal "And...?"

Joey "Then they'll jump overboard, of course...and then *splash*! Get it? Captain Splash."

Jamal "Good one. Okay, are we ready to set sail, Captain Splash?"

Joey "We've got to get supplies
before we can sail."

Jamal "Like what?"

Joey "We need to get weapons to
fight other pirates with, and we've
got to get some food, too. We might
be at sea for a really long time."

Jamal and Joey go ashore. A lady pirate, who looks a lot like Joey's mother, is working in the galley, which looks a lot like the kitchen. The lady pirate helps pack plenty of food for Captain Blood and Captain Splash.

CHAPTER 3

Blood and Guts

In the meantime, Captain Blood and Captain Splash collect a bunch of water ballons (bombs). Soon the pirates are back on board, ready to set sail.

Jamal "We need to think of a really good name for our ship."

Joey "Well, Dad's given it a name already—*Lady Breeze*."

Jamal "That doesn't sound like the name of a pirate ship. I know! We should call it *Blood and Guts*."

Joey "Yeah, much better—the *Blood and Guts*. Captained by the most feared pirates in the world: Captain Blood and Captain Splash."

Jamal "Captain Splash, we should stack our bombs at the pointy end of the ship."

Joey "That's a good idea, Captain Blood, but I think the pointy end is called the sharp end."

The ship sets sail for the open sea. The sea looks a lot like Joey's backyard.

Jamal "We've been sailing for a long time, Captain."

Joey "That's what I was thinking, Captain. Maybe we should anchor and take a lunch break? What have we got?"

Jamal opens the lunch box and looks inside.

Jamal "We've got peanut butter
sandwiches and more peanut
butter sandwiches."

Joey "Well, it's a good thing that
pirates love peanut butter."

Jamal and Joey sit down and eat
their lunch. All of a sudden a
water balloon splatters on top of
Joey's head.

Jamal "We're under attack!"

Joey "Yeah, and I'm soaked."

Jamal "No time to lose. Time to fight back."

Jamal and Joey stand up and look out to sea. In the distance is a huge wave that looks a lot like a fence.

Jamal "Whoever ambushed us must be hiding behind that big wave."

Joey "I bet it's those girl pirates from next door."

Jamal "Well, it's time to show them why boys rule—it's time to defend ourselves!"

Joey "Yeah, it's time for Captain Blood and Captain Splash to rule the seas!"

The boys race to the front of the boat and collect all the water balloons that they brought on board.

Jamal "This could be the greatest pirate war ever."
Joey "Look out, here comes another bomb. Dive for cover."

CHAPTER 4

Full-on Battle

Splash! Another water balloon explodes on the deck of the *Blood and Guts.*

Jamal "Phew! That was close. When we defeat them we'll take all their treasure."

Joey "They're only girl pirates. They haven't got any treasure that we'd want."

Jamal "Maybe they've got some food. 'Cause to be honest with you, Captain Splash, there's only so much peanut butter most feared pirates like us can eat."

Suddenly, *splat*! A scream is heard coming from behind the fence.

Joey "Yeah, got 'em! Sounds like a direct hit."

Joey throws two more bombs. Jamal throws three. There are more screams from the other side of the fence.

Jamal "I think we're gonna win this pirate war."

Joey "Yeah, *arrrrr, me hearty.* I think you're right."

Captain Blood and Captain Splash keep throwing their bombs, one after the other.

Joey "I haven't heard any more screams. Maybe they've drowned or sailed away? It's quiet—too quiet."

Jamal "Well, we'll just keep bombing them—to make sure that we really win this pirate war. Pass me another bomb."

Joey "We don't have any more bombs left—we ran out!"

Suddenly, from behind the fence the sounds of "Attack! Attack! Attack!" echo across the water.

Captain Blood and Captain Splash look worriedly at each other.

Jamal "Oh no! I think we're in big trouble."

CHAPTER 5

The White Flag

The boys crouch down and discuss their next course of action.

Joey "Don't worry, Captain Blood, 'cause the best form of defense is attack."

Jamal "Yeah, if only we had something to attack with. Look out! Here comes another one! We're gonna be hit!"

Joey *"Captain Splash, the greatest pirate ever to sail the seas, to the rescue!"*

Joey flies through the air, as if he is saving a goal in soccer and, remarkably, catches the water-filled balloon without breaking it.

Jamal "Great catch, Captain Splash!"

Joey throws the balloon back. A scream from the girl pirates can be heard across the sea. Suddenly, a stream of water-filled balloons is tossed at the boys. The boys duck for cover.

Joey "Look out, Captain Blood!"

Splash! Jamal is hit and is soaked.

Joey "Are you wounded?"

Jamal "Just a graze. It's okay, I'm Captain Blood, I'll just fight on."

Joey "Look! They're waving a white flag."

27

Jamal "That means they want to surrender. That's weird. They were winning. Maybe they've run out of bombs."

Joey "Or they're more wounded than we are. Should we ask them what they want?"

Jamal "We don't have to. Look, they're holding up a sign."

A cardboard sign appears from behind the fence. It reads, "Do you want something to eat?"

Captain Blood and Captain Splash look at each other.

Joey "I wonder what they've got to eat."

Jamal "Maybe we should invite them aboard. I bet it's good, whatever they've got."

Joey "Yeah. Okay. But once we've eaten their food we'll make them walk the plank and let the sharks eat them."

Jamal "Brilliant idea, Captain Splash. But let's find out what they've got first."

Joey "Okay. Hold on, I'll swim to shore and make a sign."

Joey runs into the house and then returns to the boat with a sign that reads, "What sort of food do you have?" He holds it up for the girl pirates to see.

Jamal "I hope it's chips or candy. Real treasure!"

A few minutes later the girls hold
up another sign. It reads, "We have
peanut butter sandwiches!" And with
that, the boys instantly lose their
appetite.

BOYZ RULE!

Pirate Lingo

Jamal

Joey

bow The front of a ship, or the pointy end.

"man overboard!" A cry for help! Somebody has fallen overboard.

poop deck The highest deck on the ship—usually above the captain's quarters.

sea legs When you get used to the rocking of a ship in the water.

stern The back of a ship, or the non-pointy end.

walk the plank When you're forced by pirates to walk out on a plank over the side of the ship and then drop into the ocean to be eaten by sharks.

33

Pirate Musts

☞ Lift the anchor before you try to sail.

☞ Wear a patch over one eye.

☞ Have a big earring in at least one ear.

☞ Learn to say "Aye aye, Captain."

☞ Carry a sword.

☞ Know how to read a compass. This is very important if you don't want to get lost in your own backyard.

☞ Carry bombs. You never know when girl pirates might attack.

☞ Make sure that you always take plenty of food along. You never know how long you might have to stay at sea.

☞ Fly a flag from your ship with the words "Boyz Rule!" written on it.

☞ Make sure you have a plank on your ship (just in case you might have to make a girl pirate walk it)—and no, don't use your mom's ironing board.

☞ Put together a treasure chest and then bury it in a secret spot.

☞ Draw a map to show where your treasure is buried—mark the spot with an "X."

BOYZ RULE!

Pirate Instant Info

💀 Pirates always fly a special flag when they are about to attack another ship.

💀 A pirate's flag has a skull and crossbones on it. The flag is called the Jolly Roger.

💀 One of the most famous pirates of all time was Blackbeard. His real name was Edward Teach and he was from England.

💀 The longest sailing race in the world is the Volvo Ocean Race. This around-the-world race starts in England, finishes in Germany, and is 32,250 nautical miles long (59,727 km).

In the classic story "Peter Pan," Peter's arch rival is an evil pirate named Captain Hook.

A favorite treasure for pirates from hundreds of years ago were doubloons, which were Spanish coins made from pure gold.

Pirate ships usually had lots of men in their crew. There weren't many women pirates.

BOYZ RULE!

Think Tank

1 What are Jamal and Joey's pirate names?

2 What is the real name of the boat? What do the boys rename it ?

3 What do you call the right side of the boat? What do you call the left side?

4 What do you call the back of a boat? What do you call the front, pointy part?

5 What do sails do?

6 Jamal and Joey play on the boat without asking permission. What do you think about this?

7 The girls next door throw water balloons at Jamal and Joey, and the boys throw some back. Do you think this is a good idea? Why or why not?

8 What should you always wear when you go sailing? Why?

Answers

1 Jamal calls himself Captain Blood and Joey calls himself Captain Splash.

2 The actual name of the boat is *Lady Breeze* but the boys rename it *Blood and Guts* for the game.

3 The right side is the starboard side and the left side is the portside.

4 The back of the boat is the stern and the front is the bow.

5 Sails catch the wind, which then helps the boat move.

6 Answers will vary.

7 Answers will vary.

8 You should always wear a lifejacket in case you fall overboard or the boat capsizes.

How did you score?

- If you got most of the answers correct then, *shiver me timbers*, you're born to be a pirate in your own backyard.

- If you got more than half of the answers correct you love to hunt for treasure, but aren't psyched about wearing a fluffy pirate shirt and patch.

- If you got less than half of the answers correct, pirate life may not be for you, but you don't mind watching pirate movies.

Felice → ← Phil

Hi Guys!

We have lots of fun reading and want you to, too. We both believe that being a good reader is really important and so cool.

Try out our suggestions to help you have fun as you read.

At school, why don't you use "Pirate Attack" as a play and you and your friends can be the actors. Set the scene for your play. Make a pirate flag and map and bring them to school to use as props, but whatever you do, don't throw any water balloons in the classroom. Pretend you and your crew are boarding an enemy ship.

So...have you decided who is going to be Jamal and who is going to be Joey? Now, with your friends, read and act out our story in front of the class.

We have a lot of fun when we go to schools and read our stories. After we finish, the kids all clap really loudly. When you've finished your play your classmates will do the same. Just remember to look out the window—there might be a talent scout from a television station watching you!

Reading at home is really important and a lot of fun as well.

Take our books home and get someone in your family to read them with you. Maybe they can take on a part in the story.

Remember, reading is a whole lot of fun.

So, as the frog in the local pond would say, Read-it!

And remember, Boyz Rule!

Felice

BOYZ RULE!
When
We Were Kids

Phil

Phil "Have you ever played pirates?"

Felice "Plenty of times. Have you?"

Phil "Yeah, and I was in a boat that sank."

Felice "That's terrible! What happened?"

Phil "I was playing pirates in my father's boat and it tipped over!"

Felice "Gee, what did you do?"

Phil "Well, I just let the boat sink to the bottom then I swam to safety!"

Felice "Gee, that must have been scary."

Phil "Yeah, it could have been if I hadn't been in the swimming pool."

BOYZ RULE!
What a Laugh!

Q How does a boat show its love?

A It hugs the shore.

43